The Very First Christmas

By Melaine Rochford

Illustrated by Anastasia Ceastichina

Published By VoiceMel

voicemel

'Twas a starry night,
and all through the hills,

shepherds were watching
their sheep in the fields.

4

When suddenly a bright angel appeared.

Everyone was afraid. They trembled in fear.

This angel had
        good news to share,

good tidings for all
        people everywhere!

"Christ The Lord has been
born today!
Go see him in Bethlehem,
get on your way!"

When suddenly more angels filled the sky.

raising their voices, lifting

God's name on high!

11

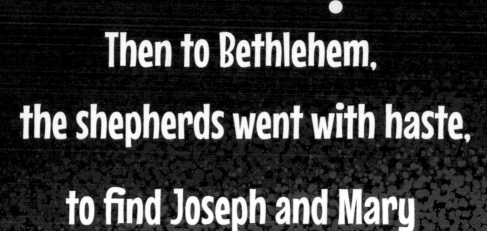

Then to Bethlehem,
the shepherds went with haste,
to find Joseph and Mary
with their little babe.

There wrapped in cloth, sleeping in a manger, was the baby boy, who is the world's Savior.

The shepherds couldn't believe
what they heard and saw.

They told everyone. People listened in awe.

17

The talk of the town was Jesus, the baby boy,
born to bring the world hope,
love, peace and joy!

Always remember Jesus is the reason for the Christmas season!

A CHRISTMAS PRAYER

Dear Lord,
You came from heaven to earth
A mighty King with a humble birth
Your love, Your peace, Your hope, Your joy
Are greater than any trinkets and toys
Help me to know You better I pray
And live my life for You everyday

Amen

23

Thank you for reading.

If you and your child enjoyed this book,

let us know at

www.voicemel.com